ÎETHKA

STORIES & LANGUAGE

IN STONEY NAKODA COUNTRY

Îethka Îabi ne

Îethka Mâkocî nen

Scan for language links

ÎETHKA

STORIES & LANGUAGE

IN STONEY NAKODA COUNTRY

Îethka Îabi ne Îethka Mâkocî nen

◆

Tatâga Thkan Wagichi (Dancing White Buffalo)
a.k.a. Trent Fox, M. Ed.

Îyâ Sa Wiya (Red Mountain Woman)
a.k.a. Valentina Fox

Illustrations: Wiyaga Wiyâ
a.k.a. Tanisha Wesley

DV **DURVILE** & **UpRoute**

CALGARY, ALBERTA, CANADA

UPROUTE IMPRINT OF
DURVILE PUBLICATIONS LTD.
Calgary, Alberta, Canada
Durvile.com

DURVILE.COM

LIBRARY AND ARCHIVES CATALOGING IN PUBLICATIONS DATA

Îethka Stories and Language in Stoney Nakoda Country

Authors: Fox, Trent. Tatâga Thkan Wagichi
Fox, Valentina. Îyâ Sa Wîyâ
Illustrations: Wesley, Tanisha, Wiyaga Wîyâ

1. Indigenous Language
2. First Nations | 3. Truth and Reconciliation | 4. Residential Schools

Watâga Wîya, Îethkaîhâ Yawabi, Îya Sa Wîyâ Wahogu-kiybi Cha, Ne Îethka Makochî Chach
were originally published in The Calgary Public Library's Treaty 7 Language Series.
These stories and teachings are reprinted with permission by The Calgary Public Library.

Spirit of Nature Series. Series editors, Raymond Yakeleya and Lorene Shyba

ISBN: 97-8-1990735-45-5 (pbk), 978-1-988824-80-2 (e-pub)
978-1-988824-58-1 (audio)

Jacket and Book design Lorene Shyba
Illustrations where indicated in the chapter Îethkahâ Yawabi were assisted by AI.
Photos in chapter Hâbâ Ririnâ, permission of The United Church of Canada

Durvile Publications acknowledges financial support for book development and production
from the Government of Canada through Canadian Heritage, Canada Book Fund
and the Government of Alberta, Alberta Media Fund.

The lands where our studios stand are a part of the ancient homeland and traditional territory of many Indigenous
Nations, as places of hunting, travel, trade, and healing. The Treaty 7 Peoples of Southern Alberta include the
Siksika, Piikani, and Kainai of the Niisitapi (Blackfoot) Confederacy; the Dene Tsuut'ina; and the Chiniki, Bearspaw,
and Wesley Stoney Nakoda First Nations. We also acknowledge the homeland of the Métis Nation of Alberta.
We commit to serving the needs of Indigenous Peoples today and into the future.

DEDICATION

Îethka: Nakoda Stories in Stoney Nakoda Country
is dedicated to the memory of dedicated scholar
Tatâga Thkan Wagichi, Dancing White Buffalo,

TRENT FOX.

CONTENTS

CONTENTS

MÂKOCHÎ NE

Tatâga Thkan Wagichi

Ahomapabisîch eyage chagach
Dûhû okadahûnâ
Kohâ dûhû othnigahûnâ
Wahniyomnî ko oda wan
Mâkochî ne zehâ sihnach
Yuchâchâhûnâ
Onâ kohûnâ
Mînî îsh opten û wan
Mâckochî ne zehâ siksach
Wodejabi ne
Nâgu thiktabin ne
Tormnârhti îko
Wanîja yabiwan
Mâkochî ne mâgidââsîch eyach
Wîchastabi ne nârhûbiktok
Ne edâhâ îyuthpebiktok
Anâroptâm
Mâkochî ne osimânam eyach

THIS LAND

Trent Fox

This land is now tired
It is saying you no longer respect me
It becomes very hot
It also becomes very cold
There are tornadoes occurring
The land is now angry
There are earthquakes
There are fires
And the water levels are changing
We have forgotten respect
The animals, the birds, the bees
are disappearing
The land is saying I am not well
Will we listen?
Or not?
Will we learn from this?
Or not?
The land is saying, "Take pity on me."

◆

ÎETHKAHÂ WAHOGÛ-WÎCHAKIYABI

Wakâ ne wachî ya.

Thudanâ ne ta-wakâ yak.

Mâkoche ne ahopa.

Wa'ahogipa.

Wogasodesîyâ îchihnuha

Snîzebinâ cha înaga.

Wayubâbigam.

Odagijiye dââbi yuha.

Nîtawachî, nîchâde ekta aîchiktaga.

Ohnîrhpa nîchiyek.

Yurhpabi nîchiyek.

Wogidâ ya.

ÎETHKA VALUES

Rely on the Creator.

Don't let money be your god.

Respect Mother Earth.

Show respect.

Embrace purity and sacredness.

Be gentle in heart and mind.

Show hospitality.

Help others without hesitation. Be obedient.

Keep your mind and heart strong.

Don't be discouraged.

Don't let others bring you down.

Keep going.

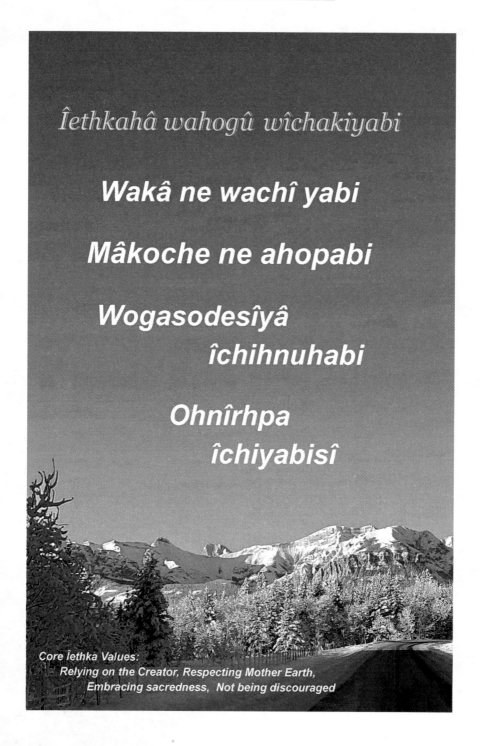

Îethkahâ wahogû wîchakiyabi

Wakâ ne wachî yabi

Mâkoche ne ahopabi

**Wogasodesîyâ
îchihnuhabi**

**Ohnîrhpa
îchiyabisî**

Core Îethka Values:
Relying on the Creator, Respecting Mother Earth,
Embracing sacredness, Not being discouraged

Photo: Trent Fox. Text: Kimberley Fox

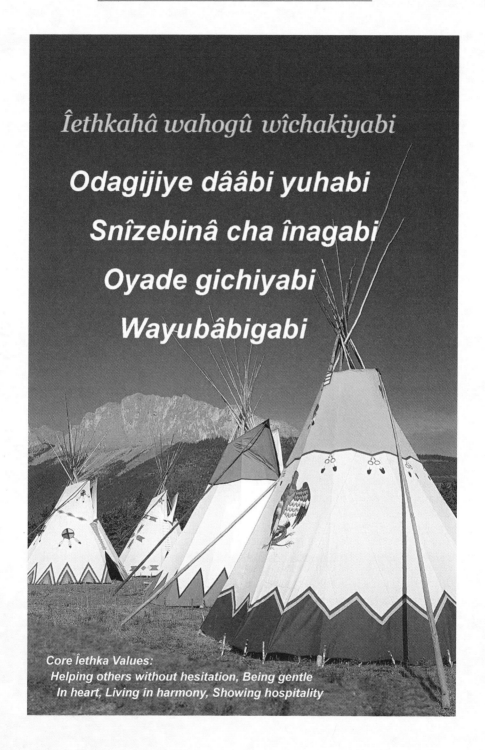

Îethkahâ wahogû wîchakiyabi

Odagijiye dââbi yuhabi

Snîzebinâ cha înagabi

Oyade gichiyabi

Wayubâbigabi

Core Îethka Values:
Helping others without hesitation, Being gentle
In heart, Living in harmony, Showing hospitality

My Three Teachings
Tatâga Thkan Wagichi (Trent Fox)

#1 Tehân togaheya
Introduction to Îethka Language
#2. Îethkahâ A's, Â's, B's ze yuthpe wîchakiyach
Grizzly Bear Woman Teaches the A's, Â's & B's
#3. Îethkahâ Yawabi
Counting in Îethka Stoney Language

Îsniyes ewîchawagiyach Richard Van Camp, Alayna Many Guns, Calgary Public Library, Dr. Lorene Shyba enâ. Owabi îgowa-bi-chiya îgogiyabi ne. Wowawe ne, mîtâgen Kim Fox ejiyabi ke awachî owawe chach. Îsniyes.

Thank you to Richard Van Camp, Alayna Many Guns, The Calgary Public Library, and Dr. Lorene Shyba at Durvile & UpRoute for helping us. These teachings are written in memory of my sister, Kim Fox Watâga Wîyâ (Grizzly Bear Woman).

Îsniyes, *Thank you*

TEHÂN TOGAHEYA
Introduction to Îethka Language

IN THIS BOOK, we turn to the Îethka language to reclaim our identity. Elder John R. Twoyoungmen teaches us that, "We speak the Îethka language. Therefore, we are Îethkabi." Elder John R. Twoyoungmen is a teacher who has studied the Îethka language since 1965.

Îethka People are also known as the Assiniboine and Stoney. As a bigger group, the Dakota, Lakota, and Nakoda People are known as the Sioux. These are terms that are not in the Îethka language. For this book, we will use Îethka to identify the Stoney Nakoda and to identify the Sioux. The word Îethka is translated as "Speaker of a clear language."

The Îethka language is spoken by the Îethka Nakoda People. The Îethka Nakoda Nation includes the Bearspaw, Chiniki, and Wesley First Nations. The Îethka Nakoda Nation has a population of over 5,200 members living in Big Horn (Wapta Mnotha), Eden Valley (Gahna) and Morley (Mînî Thnî). Îethka Nakoda People identify themselves as Îethka in our language.

Îethka hektam ubi ze Îethka, *History*

THE ÎETHKA PEOPLE have an interesting history. There are families who have lived in the foothills of the Rocky Mountains before European contact. There are also families who arrived as part of different migrations. Each family has a unique history.

The Îethka People have relatives in the Alexis and Paul First Nations. They also have relatives among the Nehiyaw (Cree). The Nehiyaw were friends of the Îethka. Many Îethka People have Nehiyaw ancestors. However, the Îethka and Nehiyaw spoke different languages.

The Canadian government wanted to integrate Indigenous children into European ways of life. They did this by taking Indigenous children from their parents and their cultures. In residential schools, Indigenous children were taught a different language and culture. However, Îethka children spoke Îethka to each other in the playground and at home. This allowed the Îethka language to survive.

Îethka Elders are still telling their stories in Îethka and there are Îethka youth who can still understand Îethka teachings. In this collection, we will learn about Îethka values. We will also learn from the wisdom of Elders and fluent speakers.

We will first learn about the Îethka alphabet. In the early 1970s, more than fifty Elders representing each band took part in developing this system as part of the Stoney Cultural Education Program. This was their legacy. In this collection, we honour their legacies. We will also learn how to count, about place names, residential school, and traditions.

Îethka Alphabet, Grammar, and Tips for Pronunciation

Scan for language links

ALPHABET

a	**ta** *moose;* **akida** *look (at it)*	**n**	**node** *throat;* **tababan** *ball*
â	**châ** *wood;* **nâbe** *hand*	**o**	**to** *blue;* **soga** *thick;* **toch** *it's blue*
b	**baha** *hill;* **owabi** *book*	**p**	**pa** *head;* **apa** *hit it*
ch	**châde** *heart;* **wathtech** *it's good*	**r**	**ri** *brown;* **horâ** *fish*
d	**dagun** *thing(s);* **wada** *boat*	**rh**	**rhokta** *gray;* **warhpe** *leaf, tea*
e	**ne** *this;* **nen** *here;* **ech** *he/she is*	**s**	**sube** *intestine;* **skada** *play*
g	**gamubi** *drum;* **châgu** *road*	**t**	**ta** *moose;* **wapta** *river*
h	**ha** *skin;* **hâ** *yes;* **hna** *go home*	**th**	**thaptâ** *five;* **wathte** *good*
i	**ti** *house;* **i** *mouth;* **tin u** *come in*	**u**	**mu** *thunder;* **uch** *he/she's coming*
î	**hî** *fur;* **thîde** *tail;* **nîbi** *life*	**û**	**ûbi** *wing;* **sûga** *dog;* **ûch** *he/she's (at)*
j	**thija** *squirrel;* **ozîja** *bear*	**w**	**woga** *grasshopper;* **wîcha** *man*
k	**ku** *give it to him/her;* **mâku** *give me*	**y**	**yaktâ** *drink (it);* **wîyâbi** *women*
m	**mîni** *water;* **amâkida** *look at me*	**z**	**zotha** *marmot;* **pezi** *hay*

VOWEL PRONUNCIATION

a about as in English *fa*t*her;* **e** in ca*fe;* **i** in *ski;* **o** in *go;* **u** in *blue;* **â**, **î**, **û** = nasalized

1. Îethka is not like English where letters can represent different sounds. Each Îethka letter represents only one sound. For example, oda (a lot) and opa (follow).
2. There are three nasal vowels in Îethka that are important to know. They are â, î, and û. It is important to understand that nasal vowels create different sounds than oral vowels.
3. Each vowel generally marks the end of a syllable. For example, dââwaûch (I am doing good) is pronounced dâ-â-wa-ûch. Keep this in mind as you go along.

How to use the Îethka writing system

It is important to know the sounds made in the Îethka language. Each sound is represented by a letter or consonant cluster. Roman letters are used represent the sounds. In Îethka, there are four consonant clusters that represent one sound. There are also eight vowels including three nasal vowels.

Consonant clusters

Ch – Chabuch (tag)

Rh – Rhorga (badger)

Th – Thaba (black)

Th – Thaptâ

Nasal vowels and oral vowels

Oral	**Nasal**
a – aba (some)	â – âba (day)
i – ibi (they went)	î – îbi (blanket)
u – u (come)	û – û (stay)

Review the Îethka alphabet and think about what sound each letter represents in Îethka. Remember that each letter represents only one sound. We will now look at that mark location in Îethka.

Determiners (Demonstratives)

In Îethka, there are five terms that help you determine what is being discussed. They are ne, ze, ke, ga, and cha.

Ne defines something that is near you.

Ze defines something that is near who you are talking to (away from you).

Ke defines something that is not visible and/or is in the past.

Ga defines something that is in the distance.

Cha defines something that you are talking about.

Ne translates to "this" and refers to something near you. An example is suwatâga ne (this horse).

Ze translates to "that" and refers to something far away from you. An example is suwatâga ze (that horse).

Ke refers to something in the past or something you cannot see. An example is suwatâga ke (a horse, in the past).

Ga translates to "that" and refers to something further away from you. An example is suwatâga ga (that horse, over there).

Borhborhâgen ne omâku – lend me this car (near you).
Borhborhâgen ze omâku – lend me that car (away from you).
Borhborhâgen ke omâku – lend me your car (not visible).
Borhborhâgen ga omâku – lend me that car (over there).

These terms are found throughout the Îethka language. These terms can stand alone. They can also be affixes to certain words:

Nedâhâ – from here
Zedâhâ – from there
Gadâhâ – from over there
Kedâhâ – from that place (not visible)

It is important to know what each means and when to use them. We will now learn about terms that mark possession.

Terms that mark possession

There are two ways to mark possession using the same word – tawaye. If you are not using miye before tawaye, you can simply say tawawach or tawayach as described when marking possession with W and Y. In this example, niye tawaye becomes tawayach. Possession can also be marked by using mî, nî, and î as prefixes as described when marking possession using these prefixes.

Owns – Tawaye   Owns - Tawaye
I own – Tawawach   I own – Mîtawach
You own – Tawayach   You own - Nîtawach
We own – Tawaîyâch   We own – Îtawach

Pay attention to wa, ya, mî, nî, and î as you read along. Remember that wa and mî indicate possession in 1st person. In 2nd person ya and nî play that role. Î is used when we own something as demonstrated:

Tûgaksiju – His/ Her grandpa   Mîtûgasin – my grandpa
Nîtugasin – Your grandpa   Îtûgasin – grandpa

Plurals in Îethka

Îethka People use two suffixes to make nouns and verbs plural. For most nouns and verbs, the term (bi) is added to the end of each word to mark plurals. For verbs that indicate command, the suffix (m) is added to mark plurals. Examples below:

Noun: Sûga (dog)   Sûgabi (dogs) Sûgabinâ (small dogs)
Verb: Mânî (walk)   Mânîbich (they are walking)
          Mânîbin (they walked)
Verb: Îyodâga (sit)   Îyodâgam (sit, all of you)
          Îyodâgabin (they sat down)

Notice that mânîbich has (ch) added as a suffix making (bi) an infix. Ch is a declarative suffix that is added to verbs to indicate something is occurring. The letter (n) is a suffix that indicates something happened in the past as in mânîbin (they walked). Note that the suffixes n and nâ can also refer to something that is small. For example, sûgabinâ (dogs) or thiktabin (small birds) as we see in the examples provided.

Common Affixes

Affixes are terms that can be added to:
Prefix – beginning of a word
Suffix – end of a word
Infix – within a word

Common affixes used in Îethka are:
Wa   awapa (I hit)   ayapa (You hit)
Mâ   amâpa (He/she hit me)   anîpa (He/she hit you)

Ch	awapach (I hit him/her)	amâpach (He/she hit me)
M	apam (Hit him/her)	amâpam (Hit me)
N	ayapen (You did hit him/her)	amâpen (He/she did hit me)
Bi	amâpabich (They hit me)	

Wa – refers to something that affects me.

Ya – refers to something that affects you.

Mâ – refers to something that affects me.

Mî – refers to something that affects me.

Nî – refers to something that affects you.

Ch – indicates something took place.

M – suffix used in verbs to indicate command.
  It also marks plurals in verbs.

Bi – suffix used in nouns and verbs to mark plurals.

N – refers to something in the past.
  It can also mark something small.

It will be helpful to remember the common affixes that change the meaning of words in the Îethka language. As you read the stories, you will notice these affixes throughout the book.

These are variations in Îethka language and pronunciation that have developed over time. As fluent speakers, the authors recognize and respect these differences.

I have brought to you a short history of Îethka People and I also offer here the alphabet, consonant clusters, nasal and oral vowels, words that help determine what is being discussed, ownership, and how words are turned into plurals. We have also learned about common affixes used in the Îethka language. Keep these in mind as you read about the alphabet, number system, body parts, place names, residential schools, and traditional teachings. We hope you have fun learning about the Îethka language in this collection.

—*Tatâga Thkan Wagichi (Trent Fox)*

Scan for a pronunciation guide.

Watâga Wîyâ

Îethkahâ A's, Â's, B's ze yuthpe wîchakiyach

Grizzly Bear Woman Teaches the A's, Â's & B's

Tatâga Thkan Wagichi
Dancing White Buffalo *(Trent Fox)*

Illustrations: Wiyaga Wiyâ (Tanisha Wesley)

21

Âba wathtech.
Tatâga Thkan Wagichi emâgiyabich.
Îethka hemâchach.

Good day.
I am called Dancing White Buffalo.
I am an Îethka person.

Âba wathtech.
Watâga Wîyâ emâgiyabich.
Îethka wîya hemâchach.

Good day.
I am called Grizzly Bear Woman.
I am an Îethka person.

Îethkabi ze Nakoda hechabich. Mînî Thnî ekta tibi chach. Aba îs Gahna nâgu Wapta Mnotha gichi ekta tibich.

Îethkabi ze Îethka îabi chach.
Ne A, Â, Bs ze ech.

The Îethka are Nakoda (Sioux).
We live at Mînî Thnî, Morley and some live at Eden Valley and Big Horn.

The Îethka People speak Îethka.
This is our alphabet.

A – A'an.
A'an ne nâzî hâch.

Crow
The crow is standing.

Â – Âba
Âba ne dââ înagam.

Day
Use this day well.

B – Baha
Mâkochi ne bahahach.

Hill
This land has many hills.

Ch – Chaba
Chaba ze châ hûyagach.

Beaver
The beaver sees some wood.

D - Daguskân

Daguskân ne zogach.

Child

This child is whistling.

E – Eti

Wapta zen kiyân etibich.

Camp

The camp is near the river.

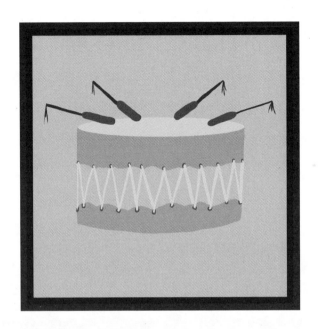

G – Gamubi
Gamubi ne ahopabich.

Drum
The drum is respected.

H – Hîhâ
Hîhâ ne îgakidagabich.

Owl
This owl is looking at us.

I – I
I ze sagiya.

Mouth
Apply lipstick to your mouth.

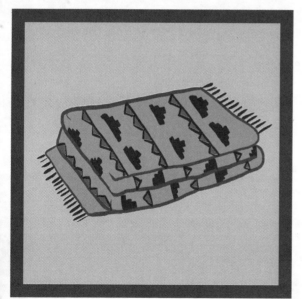

Î – Îbi
Îbi ne wathtewîch.

Blanket
This blanket is beautiful.

J - Thija

Thija ze
wayatach.

Squirrel

*The squirrel
is eating.*

K – Kiska

Kiska ze îyarhe
ekta ti chach.

Bighorn

*Bighorn sheep
live in the
mountains.*

M – Mâstîyâ

Mâstîyâ ze hnuthâhâ chach.

Rabbit

Rabbits are very fast.

N – Nowadethkan

Nowadethkan ga giyâch.

Canada Goose

The Canada goose is flying.

O – Ozîja
Ozîja ne
tâgach.

Bear
*The bear
is big.*

P – Poboktan
Poboktan ze
juthînâ chach.

Barred Owl
*The barred owl
is very small.*

R – Ri

Suwatâga ne sûri chach.

Brown

This horse is a sorrel horse.

Rh – Îyârhe

Îyârhe ga wogasodesîch.

Mountain

The mountains are sacred.

S – Sîktogeja

Sîktogeja ze
hogach.

Wolf
*The wolf
is howling.*

T – Tatâge

Tatâga ze
wasage chach.

Bison
*The bison
is strong.*

Th — Îjathebe,
Îjathebe Wapta ze.
River, *The Bow River*

Th — Wachutha, Wachutha thakwayach.
Dry Meat, I am making dry meat.

U – U
Nechagiya u.

Come
Come this way.

Û – Ûbi
Anûkathâ ga ûbi
gapepeyach.

Wings
*The bald eagle's
wings are long.*

W - Watâga

Watâga ze nechagiya mânich.

Grizzly

The grizzly is walking this way.

Y - Yazobin

Yazobin ze borâ.

Whistle

Blow the whistle.

Z – Zotha
Zotha hecha
hûmagach.

Marmot
I saw a marmot.

Maintain your Îethka language.
Remember that you are Îethka.
Take pride in being Îethka.

Îethka îabi ne hnuha ûm.
Îethka Nakoda henîchabi
ze îs gikthiya ûm.
Dââîchinabi cha îs yuham.

Questions and Answers

Watâga Wîyâ , *Grizzly Bear Woman*

Give the solutions by answering out loud:

1. What does Âba wathtech translate to in English?
2. What is the name of the main character in this story?
3. Where do the Îethka Nakoda People live today?
4. What language do the Îethka People speak?
5. What are the letters of the Îethka alphabet?
6. What are vowels in the Îethka alphabet?

On a piece of paper, match the following to their correct English translation:

1. A'an   A) Big Horn Sheep
2. Chaba   B) Owl
3. Hîhâ   C) Rabbit
4. Thija   D) Crow
5. Kiska   E) Beaver
6. Mâstiyâ   F) Squirrel
7. Nowadethkan   G) Bison
8. Ozîja   H) Wolf
9. Sîktogeja   I) Goose
10. Tatâge   J) Bear

Scan for a pronunciation guide.

Answers: 1. Good day, 2. Watâga Wîyâ (Grizzly Bear Woman), 3. Îethka Nakoda Country, 4. Îethka language, 5 & 6. Check your answers against the chart on Page 6. Matching questions. 1-D, 2-E, 3-B, 4-F, 5-A, 6-C, 7-I, 8-J, 9-H, 10-G.

Îethkahâ Yawabi

Counting in Îethka Stoney Language

Tatâga Thkan Wagichi
Dancing White Buffalo
(Trent Fox)

Wazi *(1)*. Tokân wazi (*1 fox*).

Num *(2)*. Thîde thabân nûm
(*2 black-tail deer*).

 Photos: Unless otherwise indicated, photos is this section are Creative Commons or generated by AI.

Yamni (3). Thiktabîn yamni (*3 birds*).

Ktûtha (4). Keyabi tâga ktûtha (*4 tipis*).

Photos on this page
Thiktabîn (birds): John Heerema
Keyabi tâga (tipis): Trent Fox

Thapta (5) Îyarthe thapta (5 *mountains*).

Sakpe (6). Thicha sakpe (6 *grouse*).

Sagowi (*7*). Tatâga sagowi (7 *bison*).

Sarhnora (8). Sûwa tâga sarhnora (8 *horses*).

Nâpchûwîk (9). Châohmîhmâ nâpchûwîk
(9 *wagons*).

Sakpe (*10*). Pachedên sakpe (*10 elk*).

Age Wazi (*11*). Pithên age wazi (*11 gophers*).

Age Nûm (*12*). Wobathokâ age nûm
(*12 Saskatoon berries*).

Age Yamnî *(13)*. Woya Age Yamnî *(13 flowers)*.

Age Ktûtha *(14)*. Horhâ age ktûtha *(14 fish)*.

Age Thaptâ *(15)*. Gamubi age thaptâ *(15 drums)*.

Age Sakpe *(16)*. Yarhyâîgên age sakpe *(16 stars)*.

Age Sagowî *(17)*. Châde age sagowî
(17 hearts).

Age Sarhnora *(18)*. Sûga age sarhnora
(18 dogs).

Age Nâpchûwîk (*19*). Tesna age nâpchûwîk
(19 hats).

Wîkchemnâ Nûm (*20*). Châpa wîkchemnâ nûm
(20 chokecherries).

53

Questions and Answers

Îethkaîhâ Yawabi, Counting in Îethka

The Îethka number system is simple. The numbers 1 – 10 are the most important numbers to know. For numbers 11 – 19, the term "age" is used to mean plus one, plus two. For example, age wazi is 11.

In Iethka language:

1) Count from 1 to 10.

2) Count from 10 to 20.

3) Can you count backwards from 10 to 1?

4) Count the number of eggs in the picture below:

Answers Page 1: 1. Wazi, Nûm, Yamni, Kitûha, Thapta, Sakpe, Sagowi, Sarhnora, Nâpchûwik, Wikchemnâ 2. Age Wazi, Age Nûm, Age Yamni, Age Kitûha, Age Thapta, Age Sakpe, Age Sagowi, Age Sarhnora, Age Nâpchûwik, Wikchemnâ Nûm 4. Wazi, Nûm, Yamni, Wazi.

5) Count the number of peaches in the picture below:

5) How do you say these following words in Îethka?

Fox	Gophers
Black-tail deer	Saskatoon Berries
Birds	Flowers
Tipi	Fish
Mountains	Drums
Grouse	Stars
Bison	Hearts
Horses	Dogs
Wagons	Hats
Elk	Chokecherries

Scan for a pronunciation guide.

woya, horhâ gamubi, yarhyâigén, châde, sûga, tesna, châpa.
Îyarthe, thicha, tatâga, sûwa tâga, châohmihmâ, pachedén, pithén, wobathokâ,
Age Sakpe, Age Sagowî, Age Sarhnora 6. tokân, thide thabân, thikitabin, keyabi tâga,
Nâpchûwik, Wikchemnâ, Age Wazi, Age Nûm, Age Yamni, Age Kitûtha, Age Thapta,
Page 2 Answers: 5. Wazi, Nûm, Yamni, Kitûtha, Thapta, Sakpe, Sagowî, Sarhnora,

My Three Stories
Iyâ Sa Wiyâ (Valentina Fox)

#1. Îkusin tachâ ne ayûthpe-nîkiye chach
Grandma Teaches about the Human Body

#2. Îyâ Sa Wîyâ Wahogû-kiyabi Cha
Red Mountain Receives a Teaching

#3. Hâbâ Ririnâ. *My Brown Moccasins*

Ne owabi ne aktuwa ze Noah Poucette, Îkusin ze Jenny Poucette gichi awîcha-wachî owawach. Îkusibin Flora Poucette, Mary Poucette and Maggie Hunter ebin mnehejabi ze. Îkusin Maggie en thicha ze kubi ze. Ne ebich wahogû-mâkiyabi ze.

I would like to dedicate these stories to my father, Noah Poucette, and my grandmother, Jenny Poucette.
My grandmothers Flora Poucette, Mary Poucette, and Maggie Hunter were the Elders, and Maggie Hunter was presented with the grouse.

Îsniyes, *Thank you*

#1 # Îkusin tachâ ne ayûthpe-nîkiye chach

Grandma Teaches about the Human Body

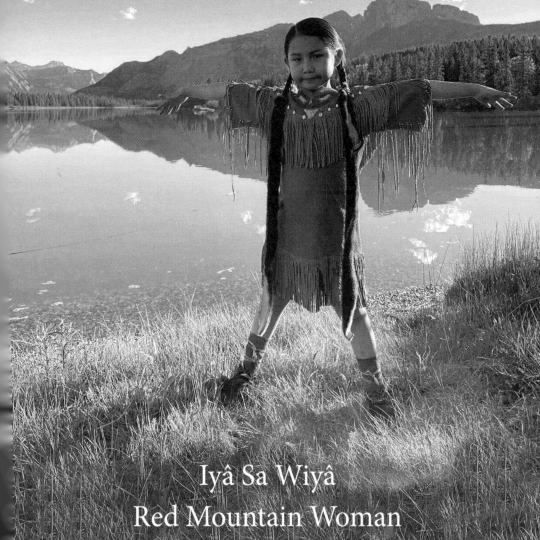

Iyâ Sa Wiyâ
Red Mountain Woman

(Tina Fox)

Âba wathtech.
Îkusin hemâchach.
Nîtachâbi ne ahogipam eyabich.

Good day,
I am Granny.
Always respect your body.

Pa.
Ne pa ze ech. Mâmân ne pa ze
kiyân awîyagabi îjenâch.

Head.
This is the head.
A baby's head must be treated carefully.

Nâdu.

Ne nâdu ze ech.

Nâdu gapepeyabi en wasagabi îge chach.

Hair.

This is the hair.

Long hair is a symbol of strength.

Nore. Ne nore ze ech. Mnehejabi
nînore wanîjek eye wahogû-îkiyabi chach.

Îtohu. Ne îtohu ze ech.
Agichide ne Îhnûhân îtohu zen owîchiwagabin.

Ear. This is the ear.
Elders teach us to listen and behave.

Forehead. This is the forehead.
Warriors sometimes paint their foreheads.

Îsta.

Ne îsta ze ech. Daguskâbin aba
îstastabi înagabi chach. Dokeyesîc.

Eyes.
These are the eyes.
Some children wear glasses and that is okay.

Porhe. Ne porhe ze ech.
Porhe ze ahnarhpam yapsakta niye chas.
Tapû. Ne tapû ze ech.
Mâmân cha tapû ze dohâ woskîge chach.

Nose. This is the nose.
Cover your nose if you are going to sneeze.
Cheeks. *These are the cheeks.*
A baby's cheeks are very cute.

I.

Ne i ze ech. Wa ahogipabi ûth i
ze îkinagam eye wahogû îkiyabi ze ech.

Mouth.
This is the mouth.
We are taught to speak respectfully.

Îsti.

Ne îsti ze ech.

Îsti zen aba putihî yuhagabin.

Chin.
This is the chin.
Some people have beards on this chin.

Tahu.

Ne tahu ze ech.

Tahu zen nâpîbin otûbi ze ech.

Neck.

This is the neck.

This is where you wear necklaces.

Hiyede.

Ne hiyede ze ech.

Hiyede ze ûth dagun yagichî hecheduch.

Shoulders.

These are the shoulders.

You can carry things on your shoulders.

Achoga.

Ne achoga ze ech.

Aba achoga zen dohâ yasîsîgabi chach.

Armpit.

This is your armpit.

Some people are very ticklish here.

Nâbejaske.

Ne nâbejaske ze ech.

Nâbejaske ne nâbe piîchiya kiye ze ech.

Wrist.

This is the wrist.

The wrist allows your hands to move.

Nâbe.

Ne nâbe ze ech. Nâbe ze ûth tano gamnabi ze ech wachutha yagarhakte chas.

Hand.

This is the hand.

You can slice meat to dry using your hands.

Nâpchoga.

Ne nâpchoga ze ech. Nâpchoga ze uth wayuthno thnobi yagarha hecheduch.

Palm.

This is the palm.

You can make pemmican balls using your palms.

Nâpûge.

Ne nâpûge ze ech. Aba ze îs îbathon, nâmpthihu, nâpthihu ogihâ, zehâ nâchasten ze.

Thumb.

This is the thumb. The rest are called pointer, middle finger, ring finger, and pinky.

Mâku.

Ne mâku ze ech. Mâku eyabi ze dagu cha kabi ze nûbagiyach. Ze mâku îs eha hecheduch.

Chest.

This is your chest. The word mâku has two meanings. It can also mean "give me" something.

Cheja.

Ne cheja ze ech.

Cheja ze ûth mâyanî ze ech.

Legs.

This is your leg.

You walk on your legs.

Tethi.

Ne tethi ze ech. Tethi rhnin awohnagabi
ze wahogû wîchakiyabi wathte chach.

Stomach.
This is the stomach.
The legend about Dirty Belly is a good teaching.

Châkpe.
Ne châkpe ze ech.
Châkpe ze, tarhâge ze, thiha ze gichi
yahneye ze ech.

Shin.
*The shin connects
your knees to your feet.*

Thiha.

Ne thiha ze ech.
Thiha zen hâba, châhâba
gichi otûbi hecheduch.

Feet.

This is the feet.

You can wear moccasins and shoes on your feet.

Thikâ.

Ne thikâ ze ech.

Thikâ ze thiha ze piîchiya kiye ze ech.

Ankle.

This is the ankle.

The ankle allows your feet to rotate.

Tawachî.

Tawachî ze ûth wanukchâ ze ech.

Tawachî wathte cha yuha.

Mind.

You think with your mind.

Have a good mind.

Îsniyes.

Akes Îkusin wayuthpe nîkiyabi chach.
Mnehejabi ahowîchagipam.

Thank You.

*Thank you. Grandma will
teach you again. Respect your Elders.*

Heavenly
Heavenly Fox, our model with her father, Joseph

Heavenly Fox's dad, photographer Joseph Fox, is father of three, and husband to Taylor Crow. They travel the powwow circuit. Joe is a Fancy Feather Dancer, Taylor is a Jingle Dress Dancer, and Heavenly is a Fancy Shawl Dancer. Joseph's older son is a Chicken Dancer and baby Michael is a dancer in training. Joseph is also a heavy equipment operator and professional driver.

Heavenly is the author Îyâ Sa Wîyâ Valentina Fox's great granddaughter.

Questions and Answers

Îkusin tachâ ne ayûthpe-nîkiye chach

1. Brown eyes are beautiful. What do we call eyes in Îethka?
2. A baby's cheeks are so cute. What do we call cheeks in Îethka?
3. Ta (Moose) have big ears. What do we call ears in Îethka?
4. Sûwatâga (Horses) have long necks. What do we call the neck in Îethka?
5. Thichâyuski uses his mind to teach lessons. What do we call the mind in Îethka?

Name these body parts in Îethka:

6.   7.   8.   9.

10.   11.   12.   13.

Answers: 1. Îsta, 2. Tâpû, 3. Nore, 4. Tahu, 5. Tawachî 6. ista 7. îtohu 8. tapû 9. Îthpathe 10. thiha 11. Nâpûge 12. Tarhâge 13. nâpchoga

 Scan for a pronunciation guide.

#2 # Îyâ Sa Wîyâ Wahogû-kiyabi Cha

Red Mountain Woman Receives a Teaching

Iyâ Sa Wiyâ
Red Mountain Woman *(Tina Fox)*
Illustrations: Wiyaga Wiyâ (Tanisha Wesley)

Âba wathtech.
Mâchaze ze Îyâ Sa Wîyâ ech.

Good day.
My name is Red Mountain Woman.

Wanîgas mâdaguskânâ zehâ, Îethkabi
ne mnogedu hâs yameye etigabin.

*A long time ago when I was a child,
the Îethka People would go on
hunt camps in the summer.*

 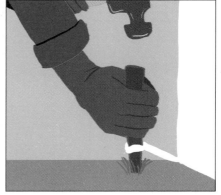

Dagugichiyabi bareîchiyabihûnâ
dokiki etiyagabin.

*Relatives would gather to go on hunting
camps in various locations.*

Wadaguwa ze,
Châ Gakthe Tibi Siya ekta etigabin.

*My relatives camped
near an old log cabin
called Châ gakthe tibi siya.*

Ehâ îkibi hâs wîyâbi ze keyabi nâgu
keyabi rhtiye ko agarhpagabin.

*When we arrived, the women would
set up the tipis and tents.*

Wîchabi ze îs mînî,
chârhâzibe ko aweya hnâgagabin.

The men would get water,
chop firewood, and prepare the camp.

Zedâhâ wîchabi ze aba,
koskabi om yameyagabin.

Then, some men and
young men
would go hunting.

Wîyâbi ze îs aba
hatha yuspiyagabin.

Some of the women
went to pick berries.

Dohâ dââgenân,
mâkochî ne gichi wazin îchinabi.
Wîjan daguskâbin dokâ
om waskaden.

*It was a lot of fun being
one with the land.*

Once, I was playing with other children.

Wanâs wîyâ cha wazi nînâ bân.
"Iyi! Thicha cha zen hiyach."

Suddenly, a woman yelled:
"There is a grouse walking by there!"

Mukabakta eyabika châânekta gapepeya
cha eyagubihûnâ tapabin.

Hoping to catch it,
they grabbed long sticks and
chased it.

Hecheyaduk thicha ze chârhâziya wosmâ cha en yeîchiyen.

However, the grouse ran under some dense willow trees.

Zen berh kuwabi ze wîchuhâ chârhâziya ze hokun yemîchiyen.

As they were loudly trying to catch it, I dashed under the willow tree.

Oksâ yeîchiyabiduk thicha
ze aîthiyâ yeîchiyen.

*They surrounded the willow tree
but the grouse was hiding.*

Thicha ze skâîhnahûnâ skâswîja
hâ hen. Ze echihâ tahu yawarhpan.
"Owaginîch" epen.

*The grouse was scared and stood still.
I quickly grabbed it by the neck and
declared, "I caught it!"*

Dââwaginen. "Miye owaginîch.
Miye mîtawach," epchen.

I was so happy. I thought the grouse
was mine because I'd caught it.

Hecheyaduk îkusin ze thicha
ze eyaguhûnâ mneheja cha kun.
Omâgapan.

However, my grandmother took
the grouse and gave it to an Elder.
I was annoyed.

Îkusin "Ne togaheyarh dagu oyaginî ze'ewan. Mneheja hecha yakuktach. Daguskânâ ne, watejage ne îs, togaheyarh dagu oginî chas Mneheja cha kubich. Ze'e chas togadam wîchârhiyabi nuhaktach" emâgiyen.

My grandmother told me:
"This is the first time you have caught something. When a child or youth first catches something, they give it to an Elder. This way, you will receive blessings in life."

Mneheja ze, thicha ze yusnasnahûnâ wahâbi cha ohân.

The Elder plucked the grouse and made grouse stew.

Wîchabi yame iyabi ke hnibichihâ
owîchagihnagabin.

*When the men returned
from their hunt, they were told
about my first catch.*

Mneheja ze chegiyahûnâ
wahâbi ke ehnen.

*The Elder then said a prayer
and served the stew.*

Îyâ Sa Wîyâ oginî chach ewîchagiyabin.

*They were told
Red Mountain Woman
caught the grouse.*

Aktuwa ze Noah, dââginen.

My father Noah was happy.

Chûhûkchu wahogûkiyabi ze,
nâgu wîchastabi wowîchaku ze.

His daughter had received
valuable teachings and fed people.

Giktiya ûgam.
Togaheyarh dagu oyaginî ze Mneheja cha
kubich. Wîcharhiyabi nuhachiyen.

So remember. Give your first catch to an
Elder to receive blessings in life.

Wîchastabi îs wowîchaku gam.

And feed people.

Questions and Answers

Îyâ Sa Wîyâ Wahogû-kiyabi Cha

Red Mountain Woman Receives a Teaching

1. What is Red Mountain Woman's name in Îethka?

2. Who was Îyâ Sa Wîyâ's father?

3. They went on hunting camps in the summer.
   How do we say summer in Îethka?

4. Where did Îyâ Sa Wîyâ's family camp?

5. What did Îethka women do when men went hunting?

6. What did Îyâ Sa Wîyâ catch?

7. What teaching did Îyâ Sa Wîyâ receive from her
   grandmother Jenny? *(You may answer in English.)*

Answers: 1. Îyâ Sa Wîyâ, 2. Noah, 3. Mnogedu 4. Châgakthe Tîbi Siya,
5. Wayuspibi 6. Thicha 7. A Îethka child's first hunt is given to an Elder.
When you provide for others, you will receive blessings in life.

 Scan for a
pronunciation
guide.

#3 # Hâbâ Ririnâ
My Brown Moccasins

Iyâ Sa Wiyâ
Red Mountain Woman *(Tina Fox)*

Illustration: Wiyaga Wiyâ (Tanisha Wesley)

Exterior of Morley Indian Residential School and
Morley Day School, ca. 1930s.

Miss Currie and the girls Social Studies class,
Morley Indian Residential School, ca. 1930s.

Hâbâ Ririnâ
My Brown Moccasins

Îyâ Sa Wîyâ emâ ech.
Wayuthpewîchakiyabi ti togaheyarh waî
ze wochigihnabikta.

*I am Red Mountain Woman. I will tell you
about my first day of school.*

Zehâgas Morley Indian Residential
School ejagabin. Daguskâbin
hechi tibis îjenâ cha gen.

*Back then, it was called Morley Indian
Residential School and children lived there.*

McDougall Orphanage and Training School for children,
Morley, Alberta ca. 1880s.

Hûguwa ze Mary hâba cha tejan
thâkthâja cha gichi mîjarhen.

My mother, Mary, made me a new pair
of moccasins and a new dress.

Amâyâbisîrh Înâ nadu mîjithûn. Zehâ Ade
gichi chuohmâ gitû amâyâbin.

Mom braided my hair before they took me.
She and my father took me to school by wagon.

Children on the steps of the Morley Residential School.
Morley, Alberta ca. 1930s.

Îna dohâ wathtenâ cha
mâhnupihûnâ dââmîchinen.

I was proud of how pretty
my mother had dressed me.

Wagiyâ Baha ako mne cha kiyân
îtigabin zehâ.

We lived by a lake behind
Eagle Hill then.

Îjathebe Wapta îs waptan hechagen.

The Bow River was a creek back then.

Baha ze thmâgan îhiyubihûnâ
wayuthpewîchakiyabi ti zen îkibin.

We came down the hill
and arrived at the school.

Ade wîyâ sijegitû cha okiyagaduk hiyomâhin.

Dad was talking to a mean-looking woman
who then came to get me.

Zehâ tin amâyen wîyâbinâ
cha dokâ nûm om.

She took me inside with two other girls.

Înâ, Ade gichi dokeyakte ze
omâgiyabiktaduk tin u cha kiyesîn.

She did not let my mom and dad
come in to tell me what was going on.

Children and staff at Morley Residential School.
Morley, Alberta ca. 1960s.

Dââgina me ke zehâ skâîhna cha mâyân.

I had been so happy to go but
now I was getting scared.

Tin îgaibichihâ îgokiyabi ka dagiye ze
thnohiyâbisin. Îethkahâ îje îgiabiwan.

When they took us inside, they talked to us but we
did not understand. We only spoke Îethka.

Children working on math at the chalkboard.
Morley, Alberta ca. 1945.

Zehâ wanâs dokâ wîyabi cha om îthnuthe
îgijiyusnosnogabin. Hâbâ Ririnâ ke ko.
Suddenly, she and two other women started taking our
clothes off. Even my little brown moccasins.

Zehâ îgithûthûbi ke mâîgikthabihûna
hakeîgichiyabin.
Then they cut off our braids and
threw them away.

Children working on math at the chalkboard.
Morley, Alberta ca. 1945.

Skaîhna îhâbi zewîchuhâ thna cha
îgabapthûbin.

*We were already scared when they
poured some type of oil on us.*

Tachâ dânârh îspâbin.
Kerosene cha hen thna ze.

*It burnt our bodies. It turned out
to be kerosene oil.*

Zehâ emâyagubihûnâ mînî nînâ rharha
cha en hukun yemâbin.
Then they took me and pushed me under
fast-running water.

Mâthpaktahâch epchen.
I thought I was going to drown.

Wîjako hecha hûmagesîwan.
I had never seen a shower before.

Zehâ thâkthâja hînîknîgenâ cha îkukubin.
Then they gave us ugly dresses to wear.

Miye ke wagichîgach hâbâ ze gichi epa ka
dagipa nâmârhûbisîn.
I asked for my new dress and moccasins,
but they did not understand.

Dagun otû îkibinâ ke îs wîja hakeîgichiyabin,
Then they threw away all our clothes.

Boys eating their lunch.
Morley, Alberta ca. 1950s.

Dââgina himu ke ze ektûth osîchina îmâhân.
Although I was happy to come,
I started to feel sorry for myself.

Rheyam wîchasta daguskâbin necha en
wîchayuzâgagabi cha he ze
thnowasîwan himu zehâ.
I did not know that they abused
Indigenous children in residential schools.

Children at writing desks with staff overseeing.
Morley, Alberta ca. 1940s.

Dagun wîjaînabi ze nâgu îgiabi ne ko îgahnustâbichiyen apiîchiyabi cha hen.

*They were working to make us lose
our culture and language.*

Anârhmân togapabi zecha aba wasiju dagiyabi ze îgogiyagabin sihnaîkiyabisîchiyaga.

*However, older students told us what the white people were
saying so we would not get in trouble.*

Teens in front of the Morley Residential School.
Morley, Alberta ca. 1940s.

Wazi wîyâ cha îs wîyâbinâ wîkoske ehâibihâs
ktûtha châ wahogûwîchakiya ko gen.
*One young woman even taught girls who reached
womanhood the rites of passage for four days.*

Ze wîyâ watejage ze Helen Beaver ejabin.
*That young woman's name
was Helen Beaver.*

Nâgâhâ nechi ze wîyâ ze dagun wîjaînabi, îgiabi ne
ko hnuhabi îgogiyabihînî epchamîgen.
I think about it now and realize how
she helped keep our culture alive.

Îsniyes ewagiyach Helen Beaver.
I thank Helen Beaver.

Hâ hechen ze dââginâ me ke hâhibichi hâ hâbâ
ririnâ ke owagicheyen. Înâ mîjarhe chan.
I was happy when I left my family but by nightfall I
thought about my experience and my moccasins and cried.
My mom had made those just for me.

Wakisîrh en ûsîn hûguwa ze.
Ze ûth dohâ wagichâptach.
My mother passed away before I went home.
This is why I regret losing my moccasins.

Reverend John McDougall, institution staff, and children who attended
McDougall Orphanage and Training School, ca. 1880s.

Rheyam wîchasta daguskâbin oda
wayuthpewîchakiye ti nechekchedu cha ibi chach.
Many Indigenous children were sent to schools like this.

Nârhârh aba tachâ yewîchayagabich. Ze ehage
îstimâbinâ ze Canada Oyade ne wîchayurhijach.
They are only just now finding bodies of some children.
In their final sleep, they have woken a nation.

Wîchoîe, *Glossary*
Îethka to English

Aba, *some*

Âba, *day*

Âba wathtech, *good day (greeting)*

Aberhen, *boiled*

Âbizihâ, *all day long*

Achoga, *arm pit*

Agarhpabin, *they covered/set up tents*

Agarhpam, *cover it*

Age, *plus*

Agichide, *warrior*

Ahîdowâgach,*is looking this way*

Ahiyaya, *singing*

Ahogipam, *respect your ...*

Ahowichagipam, *respect them*

Âîthiyâ, *ducked away*

Akes, *again*

Ako, *beyond*

Aktuwa, *my father*

Amânî, *walk on*

Amâyâbin, *they took me*

Amâyâbisîrh, *before they took me*

Amâyân, *took me*

Anârhmân, *in secret*

Anûkathâ ûbi, *bald eagle's wing*

Apiîchiyabi, *working on*

Aweya, *ready*

Awîyagabi, *to watch*

Awohnagabi, *the story*

Ayupthiyabi, *jumping*

Baha, *hill*

Bahahach, *many hills*

Baksis, *bend*

Bareîchiyabihûnâ, *by gathering*

Berh, *noisily*

Cha, *the / a* (delarative)

Châ, *wood*

Châânekta, *sticks*

Chaba, *beaver*

Châde, *heart*

Châgakthe, *cut wood*

Châgakthetibisiya, *place name referring the area where wood was cut*

Châhâba, *shoe*

Châkpe, *shin*

Châpe, *tree stump*

Chârhâzibe, *firewood*

Chârhiziya, *the willow bush*

Châwîchîpchiyân, *little pine trees*

Chegiyabi, *prayer*

Chegiyahûnâ, *by praying*
Cheja, *leg*
Chûhûkchu, *his/her daughter*
Chuohmâ, *wagon*
Chûûba, *cook*
Dââ, *good*
Dââchinabi, *pride in the self*
Dââgina, *happy*
Dââginen, *was happy*
Dââwaginen, *I was happy*
Dagipa, *what I said*
Dagiya, *what she said*
Dagiyabi, *what they say*
Dagu, *something*
Dagucha, *what*
Dagugichiyabi, *related people*
Daguginîhâsî, *is fearless*
Dagugun, *things*
Dagun, *thing*
Daguskâbin, *children*
Daguskân, *child*
Daguskânâ ne, *this child*
Dânârh, *emphatic term (overwhelm)*
Dohâ, *emphatic term (very)*
Dokâ, *other*
Dokâ om, *with others*
Dokeyakte ze, *what is going to happen*

Dokiki, *here and there*
Ebathon, *pointer*
Ech, *It is*
Echagiya û, *stay that way*
Echigiyabich, *I say to you*
Ehage, *last*
Ehâibihâs, *when reached (a place, or period in life)*
Ehâîkibiduk, *when we reached*
Ehâîkibihâs, *when we arrived*
Ehnen, *set it*
Ejabin, *was called*
Ekta, *at*
Emâ ech, *I am*
Emâgiyabich, *I am called/named*
Emâgiyen, *told me*
Emâyagubihûnâ, *she then took me*
Enûsîn, *died*
Epa, *I said*
Epchamîgen, *I have come to see*
Epchen, *I thought*
Epen, *I said*
Ethen, *soon*
Etigabin, *would camp*
Ewagiyach, *I said to him/her*
Ewichagiyabin, *were told*
Eyabika, *because they said*
Eyagubihuna, *by picking up plural*
Eyaguch, *picked up*

Eyaguhuna, *by picking up*

Eyakiye, *allow*

Eyen, *said*

Eyohas, *when he/she picks (it) up*

Gahna, *Eden Valley*

Gamnabi, *slicing (plural)*

Gapepeya, *long*

gapepeyach, *they are long*

Gapepeyacha, *long ones*

Garhchibin, *weasel*

Garhchibinâ, *a little weasel*

Gichi, *with*

Gikthiya, *remember*

Gikthiyaûgam, *so remember*

Gitu, *by*

Giyâch, *is flying*

Hâba, *moccasin*

Hâhibichihâ, *when it was dark*

Hakeîgichiyabin, *threw our (item) away*

Hakenâchihâ, *when it was morning*

Hakenârh, *early morning*

Hâs, *when (something) occurs*

Hatha, *berries*

Hechabich, *they are*

Hecheduch, *they can/that is the way*

Hechedugenâk, *so it was*

Hecheyaduk, *but then*

Hechi, *at*

Helen Beaver ejabin, *her name was Helen Beaver*

Hemâchach, *I am*

Henichabich, *you people are*

Hîhâ, *owl*

Himu ke, *I came*

Hînâpa, *appear*

Hînîgemnâ, *smell bad*

Hînîknîgenâ, *ugly*

Hînîwahnen, *I didn't like it*

Hiyede, *shoulder*

Hiyomâhin, *came to get me*

Hnâgagabin, *would set*

Hnibichihâ, *when they returned*

Hnuhabi, *retain*

Hnuhaûm, *maintain*

Hnuthâhâchach, *is fast*

Hnuzaza, *wash your*

Hogach, *is howling*

Hokun, *under*

Horha, *fish*

Horhâiptisa, *salmon*

Horhkta, *gray*

Hubakthe, *place name (also means broken bone)*

Hûguwa, *my mother*

Hûmagach, *I see*

Hûmagesîwan, *I did not see*
Hûyagach, *sees*
I, *mouth*
Îabi, *language*
Îbi, *blanket*
Îchinabi, *consider one self*
Îethka, *speaker of a clear language*
Îethkahâ, *in* Îethka
Îethkahâîje, only *in* Îethka
Îgabapthûbin, *poured on us*
Îgaga, *sitting there / are there*
Îgagichide, *we went to check*
Îgahnustâbichiyen, *to lose*
Îgaibichihâ, *when they took us there*
Îgiabi, *we speak / our language*
Îgiabiwan, *spoke*
Îgichûnîbichihâ, *we were done*
Îgijithûthûbi, *braided our hair*
Îgijiyusnosnogabin, *took off of us*
Îgiktabichihâ, *when we got up*
Îgogiyabihînî, *helped*
Îgogiyabin, *told us*
Îgokiyabika, *because they talked to us*
Îgugabin, *we would come back*
Îhâbi îchuhâ, *while standing there frightened*
Îhibihûnâ, *we came*

Îhnuhân, *sometimes*
Îhnuthe, *clothes*
Îjathebe, *bow*
Îjenâch, *must / have to*
Îkibihûnâ, *we got home*
Îkibin, *we went*
Îkinagam, *use your*
Îko, *too*
Îkubihûnâ, *they would give us*
Îkukubin, *they gave us*
Îkusin, *Grandmother*
Imahan, *became*
Înâ mîjarechan, *my mother made them for me*
Înagabin, *used*
Înagam, *use it*
Îs, *as well / too*
Îsniyes, *thank you*
Îspâbin, *it burned us*
Îsta, *eye*
Îstastabi, *glasses*
Îsti, *chin*
Îstimâbimnen, *Sleeping Lake*
Îstimâbinâ, *Sleeping*
Îthpathe, *elbow*
Îtohu, *forehead*
Îyâ, *mountain*
Îyâ Sa Wîyâ, *Red Mountain Woman*

Îyâbin, *we went*
Îyâmnâthka, *Flat Mountain*
Îyârhe, *mountain*
Îyâwîjabihûnâ, *we would go on and on*
iyi, *Oh no (female speech)*
J - Thija, *squirrel*
Junthiînâch, *is small*
Kabi, *meaning*
Keyabi, *tent*
Kidunîhe, *Kootenay*
Kiska, *bighorn sheep*
Kiyân, *close*
Kiye, *causes*
Ko, *too*
Koskabi, *young men*
Ktûtha, *four*
Ktûthachâ, *four days*
Kubich, *is given*
Kudebi, *shot at*
Kun, *gave*
Kuwabizewîchuhâ, *while they were working on (something)*
Mâchaze, *my name*
Mâdaguskânâ, *when I was a child*
Mahâdânârh, *since I went*
Mâhnîohnîhâhînâ, *dressed me up*
Mâîgikthabin, *they cut our (something) off*

Mâkochî, *land*
Mâku, *chest*
Mâku, *give me*
Mâmân, *baby*
Mamîgen, *I would go*
Mânich, *walking*
Mâstîyâ, *rabbit*
Mâstiyâmnen, *Rabbit Lake*
Mâthpaktahâch, *I will be drowned*
Mâyân, *becoming*
Mâyanî, *you walk*
Meke, *I went*
Mesîrh, *before I went*
Mîjarhen, *made for me*
Mîjithûn, *braided my hair*
Mîjiyuarben, *skinned it for me*
Mînî, *water*
Mînî nînâ rharha cha, *shower*
Mînînîn, *stream*
Mînîrhpa, *waterfall*
Mînî thnî, *Cold Water/Morley*
Mîs, *me too*
Mîstimân, *I slept*
Mîtawach, *mine*
Miye, *I or me*
Mneheja, *an Elder*
Mnogedu, *summer*
Mukabakta, *will catch*
Muthpewan, *I learned how*
Nâbe, *arm*

Nâbejaske, *wrist*
Nâchasten, *pinky*
Nâdu, *hair*
Nâgahâ, *today*
Nâgu, *also*
Nâhâ, *before*
Nâmârhûbisîn, *did not hear me / understand*
Nâpchoga, *palm of hand*
Nâpchuwîk, *nine*
Nâpîbin, *necklace*
Nâpûge, *thumb*
Nârhârh, *just now*
Nâmpthihu, *middle finger*
Nâzîhâch, *is standing*
Ne, *this*
Necha, *these*
Nechagiya, *this way*
Necheckcheducha, *things like this*
Nînâ bân, *yelled loud*
Nîtachâbi, *your bodies*
Nîyâ, *living*
Nore, *ear*
Norenîwanîjek, *listen or don't misbehave*
Nowadethkan, *Canada goose*
Nûbagiyach, *two ways*
Nuhabichiyen, *that you may have*
Nuhaktach, *you will have*
Nûm, *two*

Oda, *lots*
Ogihâ, *ring finger*
Oginîchas, *when he/she catches it*
Oginîhâch, *has caught it*
Oginîhen, *had caught it*
Ohna, *wilderness*
Ohnâ, *through*
Ohnatibi, *camping*
Oîchiwagabin, *they paint their foreheads*
Okiyagaduk, *after he talked to him/her*
Oksâ, *surround*
Okte, *loop*
Omâgapan, *I was annoyed*
Omâgiyabiktaduk, *were going to help me*
Omwati, *those I live with*
Onâchâgu, *he / she made a trail*
Osiîchina, *feel sorry for myself*
Otû, *wear*
Otûbi, *that you wear*
Owagichiyen, *I cried for my clothes*
Owaginîch, *I caught it*
Owichagihnagabin, *they would be told (details)*
Oyaginî, *you got*
Ozade, *river delta*
Ozîja, *bear*
Pa, *head*

Pacheden, *elk*
Pezimâkochî, *hayfield*
Piîchiya, *work*
Piîchiyakiye, *allows to rotate*
Pithen, *gopher*
Piyes, *despite*
Poboktan, *barred owl*
Pore, *nose*
Ptha, *reed*
Putihî, *beard*
Rhâwîn, *odorous (Cave & Basin)*
Rheyam wichasta, *Indigenous person / people of the land*
Rhteyedu, *evening*
Ri, *brown*
Riri, *brown*
Sa, *Red*
Sage, *nail*
Sagiya *make red*
Sagowî, *seven*
Sakpe, *six*
Sarhnora, *eight*
Sihnaîkiyabisîchiyaga, *so we wouldn't be scolded*
Sijegitû, *looked mean*
Sîktogeja, *wolf*
Skâîhna, *scared*
Skâîhnahûnâ, *was scared*
Skâwîjahân, *stood very still*

Sûri, *a brown horse*
Sûwatâga, *horse*
Ta, *moose*
Tachâ, *body*
Tâgach, *is big*
Tahu, *neck*
Tano, *meat*
Tapabin, *they chased it*
Tapû, *cheek*
Tarhâge, *knee*
Tatâga, *bison*
Tawachî, *mind*
Tejan, *new*
Tesnaga, *head dress*
Tethi, *stomach*
Tethirhnin, *dirty belly*
Thâkthâja, *dress*
Thamwahni, *my age*
Thânâ, *a white*
Thaptâ, *five*
Thicha, *grouse*
Thichachan, *chicken*
Thîdethaban, *mule deer*
Thijupthân, *white tail deer*
Thikâ, *heel*
Thiktaton, *little blue bird*
Thkan, *white (thing)*
Thmâgan, *come down*
Thna, *oil (kerosene)*

Thnohiyabisîn, *didn't understand*
Thnowasîn, *didn't know*
Ti, *house*
Tibichach, *live there*
Tibisîjenâgen, *had to live there*
Tibisiya, *old house / cabin*
Tibithach, *used to camp*
Tîda, *plains*
Tin, *inside*
Togadam, *in the future*
Togaheyarh, *the first time*
Togapabi, *the older ones*
Towagihâ, *lead*
U, *come*
Û, *stay there*
Ûbi, *wing*
Ûbi cha, *they were there*
Ûch, *is there*
Ûm, *be*
Ûth, *with*
Uwîchakiyesîn, *wouldn't let them in*
Waahogipabi, *respect*
Wabathîpten, *I checked*
Wachitûsî, *wild (untamed)*
Wachutha, *dry meat*
Wadaguwa, *my relatives*
Wagichâpten, *I regretted*
Wagichîgach, *I want it back*
Wagikten/Wakikten, *I woke up*
Wagiyâ Baha, *Eagle Hill*

Wahâbi, *stew*
Wahogûkiyabi, *being taught*
Wahogûwîchakiyabi, *teaching*
Wai, *I went*
Waîyate, *we ate*
Wakâmne, *Spirit Lake*
Wakisîrh, *before I got home*
Wanâs, *suddenly*
Wanîgas, *long time ago*
Wanîgaza, *long ago*
Wanûkchâ, *your thought*
Wapta, *river*
Wasagabi, *strength*
Wasagach, *is strong*
Wasiju, *white people*
Waskaden, *I played*
Wasmâ, *deep snow*
Watâga, *grizzly bear*
Watejage, *young person*
Wathtech, *good*
Wathtenâ, *pretty*
Waûch, *I am there*
Wayatach, *is eating*
Wayuthnothnobi, *pemmican*
Wayuthpenîkiyabi, *being taught*
Wayuthpewîchakiyabi Ti, *school*
Wazin, *just one*
Wichabi, *men*
Wîchagijihmûgabi, *setting snares*

123

Wîcharhiyabi, *good fortune/ blessings*

Wîchasta, *person*

Wîchastabi, *people*

Wîchawejihmûgen, *I set snares*

Wîchayurhijach, *awakened*

Wîchayuzâgabi, *abused (plural)*

Wîchispa, *Calgary*

Wîja, *all*

Wîjaînabi, *our beliefs*

Wîjako, *never*

Wîjan, *one time*

Wîkchemnâ, *ten*

Wîkoske, *young woman*

Wîyâ, *woman*

Wîyâ cha, *a woman*

Wîyâbi/Wîyâmî, *women*

Wîyâbinâ/Wîyâmînâ, *girls*

Wiyaga, *feather*

Wobathokâ, *saskatoon berries*

Wochaku, *feed*

Wochigihnabiktach, *I will tell you the story*

Woskîge, *cute*

Wosmâ, *bushy*

Yagarhacheduch, *you can make*

Yagarhaktechas, *when you will make*

Yagichî, *carry*

Yahne, *connect*

Yaktâ, *drink*

Yaktâhâch, *standing there drinking*

yakuktach, *you will give*

Yame, *hunt*

Yameyabi, *hunting*

Yameyagabin, *would go hunting*

Yamnî, *three*

Yapsaktes, *when you are going to sneeze*

Yasîsîgabin, *are ticklish*

Yawabi, *counting*

Yawarhpan, *I grabbed it*

Yecha, *going*

Yeîchiya, *go there*

Yeîchiyen, *went there*

Yemâbin, *sent me (threw me)*

Yemîchiyen, *ducked under*

Yewîchayagabich, *being found*

Yuarhba, *skin*

Yude, *eat*

Yuhagabin, *they would have*

Yuham, *keep (plural)*

Yusnasnan, *plucked feathers*

Yuspiyagabin, *went to pick*

Yuthpemâkiyen, *taught me*

Ze, *that*

Ze echas, *as a result*

Ze echihâ, *so*

Ze ektûth, *by then*
Zechi, *there noisily*
Zedâhâ, *then*
Zehâ, *then*
Zehâgas, *at that time*

Zen, *there*
Zogach, *is whistling*
Zotha, *marmot*

Glossary, Wîchoîe
English to Îethka

Abused (plural), Wîchayuzâgabi

After he talked to him/her, Okiyagaduk

Again, Akes

Age (my age), Thamwahni

All, Wîja

All day long, Âbizihâ

Allow, Eyakiye

Also, Nâgu

Am (I am), Emâ ech

Am (I am), Hemâchach

Annoyed (I was annoyed), Omâgapan

Appear, Hînâpa

Arm, Nâbe

Arm pit, Achoga

As a result, Ze echas

As well / too, Îs

At, Ekta

At, Hechi

At that time, Zehâgas

Ate (we ate), Waîyate

Awakened, Wîchayurhijach

Baby, Mâmân

Bald Eagle wing, Anûkathâ ûbi

Barred owl, Poboktan

Be, Ûm

Bear, Ozîja

Beard, Putihî

Beaver, Chaba

Became, Imahan

Because they said, Eyabika

Because they talked to us, Îgokiyabika

Becoming, Mâyân

Before, Nâhâ

Before I got home, Wakisîrh

Before I went, Mesîrh

Before they took me, Amâyâbisîrh

Beliefs (our beliefs), Wîjaînabi

Bend, Baksis

Berries, Hatha

Beyond, Ako

Big (is big), Tâgach

Bighorn sheep, Kiska

Bison, Tatâga

Blanket, Îbi

Bodies (your bodies), Nîtachâbi

Body, Tachâ

Boiled, Aberhen

Bow, Îjathebe

Braided my hair, Mîjithûn

Braided our hair, Îgijithûthûbi

Brown, Ri

Brown, Riri

Brown horse, Sûri

Burned (it burned us), Îspâbin

Bushy, Wosmâ

But then, Hecheyaduk

By, Gitu

By then, Ze ektûth

Calgary, Wîchispa

Called (was called), Ejabin

Came (I came), Himu ke

Came (we came), Îhibihûnâ

Came to get me, Hiyomâhin

Camp (used to camp), Tibithach

Camp (would camp), Etigabin

Camping, Ohnatibi

Canada goose, Nowadethkan

Carry, Yagichî

Catch (when he/she catches it), Oginîchas

Catch (will catch), Mukabakta

Caught (I caught it), Owaginîch

Causes, Kiye

Check (we went to check), Îgagichide

Checked (I checked), Wabathîpten

Cheek, Tapû

Chest, Mâku

Chicken, Thichachan

Child, Daguskân

Child (this child), Daguskânâ ne

Children, Daguskâbin

Chin, Îsti

Close, Kiyân

Clothes, Îhnuthe

Cold Water / Morley, Mînî thnî

Come, U

Come back (we would come back), Îgugabin

Come down, Thmâgan

Come to see (I have come to see), Epchamîgen

Connect, Yahne

Consider one self, Îchinabi

Cook, Chûûba

Counting, Yawabi

Cover it, Agarhpam

Cried (I cried for my clothes), Owagichiyen

Cut wood, Châgakthe

Cute, Woskîge

Daughter (his/her daughter), Chûhûkchu

Day, Âba

Deep snow, Wasmâ

Despite, Piyes

Did not hear me / understand, Nâmârhûbisîn

Did not like (I didn't like it), Hînîwahnen

Did not see (I did not see), Hûmagesîwan

Didn't know, Thnowasîn

Didn't understand, Thnohiyabisîn

Died, Enûsîn

Dirty belly, Tethirhnin

Done (we were done), Îgichûnîbichihâ

Dress, Thâkthâja

Dressed me up, Mâhnîohnîhâhînâ

Drink, Yaktâ

Drown (I will drown), Mâthpaktahâch

Dry meat, Wachutha

Ducked away, Âthiyâ

Ducked under, Yemîchiyen

Eagle Hill, Wagiyâ Baha

Ear, Nore

Early morning, Hakenârh

Eat, Yude

Eating (is eating), Wayatach

Eden Valley, Gahna

Eight, Sarhnora

Elbow, Îthpathe

Elder (an), Mneheja

Elk, Pacheden

Emphatic term (overwhelm), Dânârh

Emphatic term (very), Dohâ

Evening, Rhteyedu

Eye, Îsta

Fast (is fast), Hnuthâhâchach

Father (My father), Aktuwa

Fearless (is fearless), Daguginîhâsî

Feather, Wiyaga

Feed, Wochaku

Feel sorry for myself, Osiîchina

Firewood, Chârhâzibe

First time, Togaheyarh

Fish, Horha

Five, Thaptâ

Flat Mountain, Îyâmnâthka

Flying (is flying), Giyâch

Forehead, Îtohu

Found (being found), Yewîchayagabich

Four, Ktûtha

Four days, Ktûthachâ

Future (in the future), Togadam

Gathering (by gathering), Bareîchiyabihûnâ

Gave, Kun

Girls, Wîyâbinâ/Wîyâmînâ

Give (They would give us),

Îkubihûnâ

Give me, Mâku

Given (is given), Kubich

Glasses, Îstastabi

Go (I would go), Mamîgen

Go there, Yeîchiya

Going, Yecha

Good, Dââ

Good, Wathtech

Good day (greeting), Âba wathtech

Good fortune/blessings, Wîcharhiyabi

Gopher, Pithen

Grabbed (I grabbed it), Yawarhpan

Grandmother, Îkusin

Grey, Horhkta

Grizzly bear, Watâga

Grouse, Thicha

Had caught it, Oginîhen

Had to live there, Tibisîjenâgen

Hair, Nâdu

Happy, Dââgina

Happy (I was happy), Dââwaginen

Happy (was happy), Dââginen

Has caught it, Oginîhâch

Have (they would have), Yuhagabin

Hayfield, Pezimâkochî

Head, Pa

Head dress, Tesnaga

Heart, Châde

Heel, Thikâ

Help (were going to help me), Omâgiyabiktaduk

Helped, Îgogiyabihînî

Her name was Helen Beaver, Helen Beaver ejabin

Here and there, Dokiki

Hill, Baha

Home (we got home), Îkibihûnâ

Horse, Sûwatâga

House, Ti

Howling (is howling), Hogach

Hunt, Yame

Hunt (would go hunting), Yameyagabin

Hunting, Yameyab

I or me, Miye

I said to him/her, Ewagiyach

Îethka (in Îethka), Îethkahâ

Indigenous person/People of the land, Rheyam wichasta

Inside, Tin

It is, Ech

Jumping, Ayupthiyabi

Just now, Nârhârh

Just one, Wazin

Keep (plural), Yuham
Knee, Tarhâge
Kootenay, Kidunîhe
Land, Mâkochî
Language, Îabi
Last, Ehage
Lead, Towagihâ
Learned (I learned how),
Muthpewan
Leg, Cheja
Listen or don't misbehave,
Norenîwanîjek
Little blue bird, Thiktaton
Little pine trees, Châwîchîpchiyân
Little weasel, Garhchibinâ
Live there, Tibichach
Living, Nîyâ
Long, Gapepeya
Long ago, Wanîgaza
Long ones, Gapepeyacha
Long time ago, Wanîgas
Looking this way, Ahîdowâgach
Loop, Okte
Lose (to lose), Îgahnustâbichiyen
Lots, Oda
Made for me, Mîjarhen
Maintain, Hnuhaûm
Make red, Sagiya
Many hills, Bahahach

Marmot, Zotha
Me too, Mîs
Mean (looked mean), Sijegitû
Meaning, Kabi
Meat, Tano
Men, Wichabi
Men (young men), Koskabi
Middle finger, Nâmpthihu
Mind, Tawachî
Mine, Mîtawach
Moccasin, Hâba
Moose, Ta
Mother (my mother), Hûguwa
Mountain, Îyâ
Mountain, Îyârhe
Mouth, I
Mule deer, Thîdethaban
Must/have to, Îjenâch
My mother made them for me, Înâ
mîjarechan
Nail, Sage
Name (my name), Mâchaze
Named (I am called/named),
Emâgiyabich
Neck, Tahu
Necklace, Nâpîbin
Never, Wîjako
New, Tejan
Nine, Nâpchuwîk

Noisily, Berh
Nose, Pore
Odorous (Cave & Basin), Rhâwîn
Oh no (female speech), iyi
Oil (kerosene), Thna
Old house/cabin, Tibisiya
Older ones, Togapabi
On and on (we would go on and on), Îyâwîjabihûnâ
One time, Wîjan
Only in Îethka, Îethkahâîje
Other, Dokâ
Owl, Hîhâ
Palm of hand, Nâpchoga
Pemmican, Wayuthnothnobi
People, Wîchastabi
Person, Wîchasta
Person (young person), Watejage
Pick (went to pick), Yuspiyagabin
Pick up (when he/she picks it up), Eyohas
Picked up, Eyaguch
Picking up (by picking up, plural), Eyagubihuna
Picking up (by picking up), Eyaguhuna
Pinky finger, Nâchasten
Place name (also means broken bone), Hubakthe

Place name (referring the area where wood was cut), Châgakthetibisiya
Plains, Tîda
Played (I played), Waskaden
Plucked feathers, Yusnasnan
Plus, Age
Pointer, Ebathon
Poured on us, Îgabapthûbin
Prayer, Chegiyabi
Praying (by praying), Chegiyahûnâ
Pretty, Wathtenâ
Pride in the self, Dââchinabi
Rabbit, Mâstîyâ
Rabbit Lake, Mâstiyâmnen
Ready, Aweya
Red, Sa
Red Mountain Woman, Îyâ Sa Wîyâ
Reed, Ptha
Regret (I regretted), Wagichâpten
Related people, Dagugichiyabi
Relatives (my relatives), Wadaguwa
Remember, Gikthiya
Remember (so remember), Gikthiyaûgam
Respect, Waahogipabi
Respect them, Ahowichagipam

Respect your…, Ahogipam
Retain, Hnuhabi
Ring finger, Ogihâ
River, Wapta
River delta, Ozade
Rotate, Piîchiyakiye
Said, Eyen
Said (I said), Epa
Said (I said), Epen
Salmon, Horhâiptisa
Saskatoon berries, Wobathokâ
Say (I say to you), Echigiyabich
Scared, Skâîhna
Scared (was scared), Skâîhnahûnâ
School, Wayuthpewîchakiyabi Ti
Secret (in secret), Anârhmân
See (I see), Hûmagach
Sees, Hûyagach
Sent me (threw me), Yemâbin
Set (would set), Hnâgagabin
Set it, Ehnen
Setting snares, Wîchagijihmûgabi
Seven, Sagowî
Shin, Châkpe
Shoe, Châhâba
Shot at, Kudebi
Shoulder, Hiyede
Shower, Mînî nînâ rharha cha
Since I went, Mahâdânârh

Singing, Ahiyaya, singing
Sitting there/are there, Îgaga
Six, Sakpe
Skin, Yuarhba
Skinned it for me, Mîjiyuarben
Sleeping, Îstimâbinâ
Sleeping Lake, Îstimâbimnen
Slept (I slept), Mîstimân
Slicing (plural), Gamnabi
Small (is small), Junthiînâch
Smell bad, Hînîgemnâ
Snares (I set snares), Wîchawejihmûgen
So, Ze echihâ
So it was, Hechedugenâk
So we wouldn't be scolded, Sihnaîkiyabisîchiyaga
Some, Aba, some
Something, Dagu
Sometimes, Îhnuhân
Soon, Ethen
Speak (we speak/our language), Îgiabi
Speaker of a clear language, Îethka
Spirit Lake, Wakâmne
Spoke, Îgiabiwan
Squirrel, Thija
Standing (is standing), Nâzîhâch
Standing there drinking,

Yaktâhâch

Stay that way, Echagiya û

Stay there, Û

Stew, Wahâbi

Sticks, Châânekta, sticks

Stomach, Tethi

Stood very still, Skâwîjahân

Story, Awohnagabi

Story (I will tell you the story), Wochigihnabiktach

Stream, Mînînîn

Strength, Wasagabi

Strong (is strong), Wasagach

Suddenly, Wanâs

Summer, Mnogedu

Surround, Oksâ

Taught (Being taught), Wahogûkiyabi

Taught (Being taught), Wayuthpenîkiyabi

Taught me, Yuthpemâkiyen

Teaching, Wahogûwîchakiyabi

Ten, Wîkchemnâ

Tent, Keyabi

Thank you, Îsniyes

That, Ze

That you may have, Nuhabichiyen

That you wear, Otûbi

The/a (declarative), Cha

Then, Zedâhâ

Then, Zehâ

There, Zen

There (I am there), Waûch

There (is there), Ûch

There noisily, Zechi

These, Necha

They are, Hechabich

They are long, gapepeyach

They can/that is the way, Hecheduch

They chased it, Tapabin

They covered/set up tents, Agarhpabin

They cut our (something) off, Mâîgikthabin

They gave us, Îkukubin

They paint their foreheads, Oîchiwagabin

They were there, Ûbi cha

They would be told (details), Owîchagihnagabin

Thing, Dagun

Things, Dagugun

Things like this, Necheckcheducha

This, Ne

This way, Nechagiya

Those I live with, Omwati

Thought (I thought), Epchen

Thought (your thought), Wanûkchâ

Three, Yamnî

Threw our (item) away, Hakeîgichiyabin

Through, Ohnâ

Thumb, Nâpûge

Ticklish, Yasîsîgabin

Today, Nâgahâ

Told (were told), Ewichagiyabin

Told me, Emâgiyen

Told us, Îgogiyabin

Too, Îko

Too, Ko

Took me, Amâyân

Took me (They took me), Amâyâbin

Took off of us, Îgijiyusnosnogabin

Trail (he/she made a trail), Onâchâgu

Tree stump, Châpe

Two, Nûm

Two ways, Nûbagiyach

Ugly, Hînîknîgenâ

Under, Hokun

Use it, Înagam

Use your, Îkinagam

Used, Înagabin

Wagon, Chuohmâ

Walk (you walk), Mâyanî

Walk on, Amânî

Walking, Mânich

Want it back (I want it back), Wagichîgach

Warrior, Agichide

Wash (wash your), Hnuzaza

Watch (to watch), Awîyagabi

Water, Mînî

Waterfall, Mînîrhpa

Wear, Otû

Weasel, Garhchibin

Went (I went), Meke

Went (I went), Wai

Went (we went), Îkibin

Went (we went), Îyâbin

Went there, Yeîchiyen

What, Dagucha

What I said, Dagipa

What is going to happen, Dokeyakte ze

What she said, Dagiya

What they say, Dagiyabi

When (something) occurs, Hâs

When I was a child, Mâdaguskânâ

When it was dark, Hâhibichihâ

When it was morning, Hakenâchihâ

When reached (a place, or period

in life), Ehâibihâs

When they returned, Hnibichihâ

When they took me, Emâyagubihûnâ

When they took us there, Îgaibichihâ

When we arrived, Ehâîkibihâs

When we got up, Îgiktabichihâ

When we reached, Ehâîkibiduk

When you are going to sneeze, Yapsaktes

When you will make, Yagarhaktechas

While standing there frightened, Îhâbi îchuhâ

While they were working on (something), Kuwabizewîchuhâ

Whistling (is whistling), Zogach

White, Thânâ

White (thing), Thkan

White people, Wasiju

White tail deer, Thijupthân

Wild (untamed), Wachitûsî

Wilderness, Ohna

Willow bush, Chârhiziya

Wing, Ûbi

With, Gichi

With, Ûth

With others, Dokâ om

Woke (I woke up), Wagikten/ Wakikten

Wolf, Sîktogeja

Woman, Wîyâ

Woman, Wîyâ cha

Woman (young woman), Wîkoske

Women, Wîyâbi/Wîyâmî

Wood, Châ, wood

Work, Piîchiya

Wouldn't let them in, Uwîchakiyesîn

Wrist, Nâbejaske

Yell, Nînâ bân

You can make, Yagarhacheduch

You got, Oyaginî

You people are, Henichabich

You will give, yakuktach

You will have, Nuhaktach

ACKNOWLEDGEMENTS
TO THE LEGACY

In the 1970s, more than fifty Elders representing each
Stoney (Îethka) Nakoda band — Bearspaw, Chiniki, Wesley —
took part in developing this Îethka language system as part of
the Stoney Cultural Education Program.
We honour the Elders those whose legacy we follow including:

Charlie Abraham, John Abraham, Morgan Abraham,
Myron Baptiste, Rachel Baptiste, Claude Wesley-Beaver,
Isaac Beaver, Linda Chiniki, Mary Jane Chiniki,
Isaiah Crawler, Jack Crawler, Shirley Crawler,
George Ear, Kent Fox, Tina Fox, Wilfred Fox,
Willie Goodstoney, Dale House, Jacob House, Mary House,
Clifford Jimmy John, Jimmy Kaquitts, John Mark,
Georgia Mark, Paul Mark, Eunice Mark, Rod Mark,
Bill McLean, Tatâga Mânî, John Poucette,
Sykes Powderface, Jake Rabbit, Tom Snow,
Alvin Twoyoungmen, Elaine Twoyoungmen,
John R. Twoyoungmen, Morley Twoyoungmen,
Clarence Wesley, John Wesley, Lazarus Wesley, Lily Wesley,
Buddy Wesley, and Una Wesley.

OTHER TITLES IN THE INDIGENOUS SPIRIT OF NATURE SERIES

SERIES EDITORS: RAYMOND YAKELEYA & LORENE SHYBA

PUBLISHING AUTHORS WHO HAVE THE AMBITION TO BRING TRADITIONAL KNOWLEDGE TO THE WORLD

**THE TREE BY THE
WOODPILE**
By Raymond Yakeleya
ISBN: 9781988824031

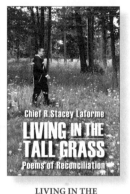

**LIVING IN THE
TALL GRASS**
By Chief R. Stacey Laforme
ISBN: 9781988824055

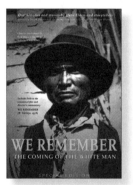

**WE REMEMBER
SPECIAL EDITION**
Eds. Stewart & Yakeleya
ISBN: 9781988824635

**STORIES OF
METIS WOMEN**
Eds. Oster & Lizee
ISBN: 9781988824215

**NAHGANNE TALES OF THE
NORTHERN SASQUATCH**
By Red Grossinger
ISBN 9781988824598

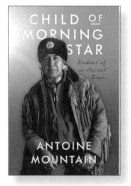

**CHILD OF MORNING STAR
EMBERS OF AN ANCIENT DAWN**
By Antoine Mountain
ISBN: 9781990735103

OTHER TITLES IN THE INDIGENOUS SPIRIT OF NATURE SERIES

SERIES EDITORS: RAYMOND YAKELEYA & LORENE SHYBA

PUBLISHING AUTHORS WHO HAVE THE AMBITION TO BRING TRADITIONAL KNOWLEDGE TO THE WORLD

**LILLIAN & KOKOMIS
THE SPIRIT OF DANCE**
By Lynda Partridge
ISBN: 9781988824277

**WHY ARE YOU STILL
HERE?: A LILLIAN MYSTERY**
By Lynda Partridge
ISBN: 9781988824826

SIKSIKAITSITAPI: STORIES
OF THE **BLACKFOOT PEOPLE**
By Payne Many Guns *et al*
ISBN: 9781988824833

**THE RAINBOW, THE
MIDWIFE, & THE BIRDS**
By Raymond Yakeleya
ISBN: 9781988824574

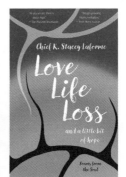

**MIDNIGHT STORM
MOONLESS SKY**
By Alex Soop
ISBN: 9781990735127

**WHISTLE AT NIGHT
AND THEY WILL COME**
By Alex Soop
ISBN: 9781990735301

**LOVE LIFE LOSS
AND A LITTLE BIT OF HOPE**
By Chief R. Stacey Laforme
ISBN: 9781990735431

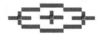

Tatâga Thkan Wagichi
(Dancing White Buffalo)
a.k.a. Trent Fox, M. Ed.

Tatâga Thkan Wagichi was a member of the Wesley First Nation, Stoney Nakoda Nation. He was completing his doctorate in Education at the University of Calgary. His inquiry was on the history of the Îethka Nakoda People and development of the Îethka language. Tatâga Thkan Wagichi passed away in 2023.

Îyâ Sa Wiya
(Red Mountain Woman)
a.k.a. Valentina Fox

Îyâ Sa Wîyâ (Red Mountain Woman) is a member of the Wesley First Nation, Stoney Nakoda Nation. A great-grandmother, grandmother, and mother, she is also a counsellor and Elder at Nakoda Elementary School. A former Certified Nursing Assistant (Practical Nurse), she earned her undergraduate degree in First Nations counselling. Tina is also a passionate advocate for the retention of the Îethka language and has contributed to language curriculum development, recording stories, and now writing in her language. Together with her family, Tina sponsors the Watâga Wîyâ Language Award at Morley Community School to encourage language learning in memory of her late daughter, Kim Fox and late son Trent Fox.